DATE DUE

DEMCO 38-296

Jenny Come Along

Adapted by
Debbie Driscoll

Illustrated by
Susan Winter

A Doubleday Book for Young Readers

AUTHOR'S NOTE

There is a traditional American folk song called "Johnny Get Your
Gun" that I heard as a little girl growing up in the Blue Ridge
Mountains of North Carolina. I used the rhythm and music from
that song, but wrote all new words. The result is "Jenny Come
Along," featuring a lively little girl who explores, mimics, and plays
her way through the day.

A Doubleday Book for Young Readers
Published by Delacorte Press
Bantam Doubleday Dell Publishing Group, Inc.
1540 Broadway
New York, New York 10036
Doubleday and the portrayal of an anchor with a dolphin are trademarks of Bantam Doubleday
Dell Publishing Group, Inc.
Text copyright © 1995 by Debbie Driscoll
Illustrations copyright © 1995 by Susan Winter   .

Library of Congress Cataloging in Publication Data
Driscoll, Debbie.
Jenny come along / adapted by Debbie Driscoll; illustrated by Susan Winter.
p.   cm.
Summary: A lively little girl romps through a variety of daily activities to the rhythm of a
traditional American folk song.
ISBN 0-385-32054-X
[1. Girls—Fiction.]   I. Winter, Susan, ill.   II. Title.
PZ7.D7874Je 1995   [E]—dc20   94-17381   CIP   AC

Manufactured in the United States of America

May 1995

10 9 8 7 6 5 4 3 2 1

For my own three busy boys,
Lane, Max, and Fletcher,
who ask the question "Why is it
that kids don't ever like to take naps,
but grown-ups always do?"

D.D.

For Eunice, with love

S.W.

Jenny get your comb,
and your cup,
and your toothbrush.

Jenny come along wake up with me.

Jenny get your shirt,
and your socks,
and your pants on.

Jenny come along get dressed with me.

Jenny get your sand,
and your pail,
and your shovel.

Jenny come along and dig with me.

Jenny get your trucks,
and your cars,
and your school bus.

Jenny come along and drive with me.

Jenny get your boots,
and your hat,
and your slicker.

Jenny come along and splash with me.

Jenny get your juice,
and your cheese,
and your crackers.

Jenny come along and eat with me.

Jenny get your broom,
and your sponge,
and your towel.

Jenny come along and clean with me.

Jenny get your toes,
and your tummy,
and your tickles.

Jenny come along and laugh with me.

Jenny get your wood,
and your nails,
and your hammer.

Jenny come along and build with me.

Jenny get your spoon,
and your bowl,
and your flour.

Jenny come along and bake with me.

Jenny get your bell,
and your drum,
and your whistle.

Jenny come along and march with me.

Jenny get your book,
and your thumb,
and your blanket.

Jenny come along and read with me.

Jenny get your bear,
and your love,
and your kisses.

Jenny come along and hug with me.

Jenny get your moon,
and your yawn,
and your pillow.

Jenny come along and dream with me.

Jenny Come Along

(Adaptation of a traditional American folk song)

Jen - ny get your comb, and your cup, and your tooth - brush.

Jen - ny come a - long, wake up with me.

2. Jenny get your shirt,
   and your socks,
   and your pants on.
   Jenny come along get dressed with me.

3. Jenny get your sand,
   and your pail,
   etc.